For God
So Loves . . .

978-0-8054-4635-7

Published by B&H Publishing Group

Nashville, Tennessee

Cover and Interior Illustrations by Glin Dibley

Illustrations copyright © 2010 by Glin Dibley

Dewey Decimal Classification: F

Subject Heading: SALVATION—FICTION \ REGENERATION

(CHRISTIANITY)—FICTION

Unless otherwise noted, Scripture quotations are from
the Holy Bible, New International Version, copyright ©
1973, 1978, 1984 by International Bible Society.

1 2 3 4 5 6 7 8 9 • 14 13 12 11 10

KNOWING, SHOWING, GROWING,

My John 3:16 DISCOVERY Book

by
Robert J. Morgan

DEDICATED TO

Victoria,
Hannah,
& Grace
who taught me all I know
about Milly, Molly, and Mary

INTRODUCTION

A Letter for Adults / vi

INTRODUCTION:
A LETTER FOR ADULTS

"I don't know if my child has received Christ as Savior, and I'm not sure what to do."

"I think my son asked Jesus into his heart last year, but he hasn't been baptized. Should I bring it up, or wait for him to mention it?"

"My granddaughter was baptized recently, but how can I encourage her spiritual growth?"

If you're asking questions like those, this book is for you!

Jesus put things simply. "For God so loved the world," He said, "that He gave His one and only Son, that whoever believes in Him shall not perish but have eternal life" (John 3:16). Even young children can understand that, for Jesus later added, "Let the little children come to me, and do not hinder them, for the kingdom of heaven belongs to such as these" (Matthew 19:14). Some of "these," however, may be hindered by our awkwardness in leading them to Christ. *Knowing, Showing, Growing: My John 3:16 Discovery Book* will reduce the stiffness, enabling you to guide your children, naturally and simply, to:

Receive Christ as Savior
Follow Him in baptism
Begin the basic habits of the Christian life

This book is primarily written for elementary-aged children. If your youngsters are preschoolers, they will need help through these lessons. Even if they are older, take an active role in working through this book with them. Your involvement shows them the priority of Christ in your life. If you take it seriously, they will. Here's how:

1. **Choose a time** when your child is alert, and approach this book with interest, fun, and a sense of importance. I suggest a definite half-hour each week for ten weeks, covering one lesson per session. Most chapters can be covered in thirty minutes or less.

2. **Begin by reading** each lesson's opening story to your child, or have him or her read it to you. Then gently oversee your child's working through each question or project.

3. **Look up each verse** with your child.

4. **Commend your child** for correct responses, and provide assistance with reassurance when he or she is unclear about the material.

5. **End each session by praying** with your child. If the lesson calls for memory work, make it a joint project.

A suggested prayer in chapter 2 can be used in leading your child to Christ. Many youngsters will be ready to pray it as their own, having worked through the preceding material. Don't pressure your children to receive Christ, but be ready to encourage them if they seem interested. After they have prayed, have them sign and date their names in the provided spaces. In future years they will treasure these records of their conversions.

A lesson is included about baptism. After studying this material, if your children want to be baptized, please make an appointment with your minister. Baptismal policies and procedures vary from church to church. Your pastor will be glad to meet with you and your child to discuss this meaningful step.

The lessons about prayer and daily Bible reading will be most effective if your youngsters see you enjoying your daily devotions. A book like this can stress the importance of a daily quiet time, but nothing replaces the model of a mom who prays, or of a dad who cherishes the Word of God.

You may want to use these lessons in a small group evangelism/discipleship course with children, or with children attending jointly with their parents. But spend sufficient time in every session with each child to ensure clarity and to convey individual love.

A cursory knowledge of Christianity is presupposed. If you are working with a child who has never heard the name "Jesus," or who doesn't know what a Bible or a church building is, you will want to be sensitive to his or her need for foundational information.

God bless you and your children as you "bring them up in the training and instruction of the Lord" (Ephesians 6:4).

PART 1: KNOWING

1. MARY MOTLEY MEETS A PRINCESS

Eight-year-old Mary Motley discovered something in the park one day. She learned that some people liked her and some loved her. But some didn't care for her at all!

She made this discovery one evening after supper when her father took her to the playground. The sun, low in the horizon, tinged the sky with traces of orange. The air smelled of autumn. The park bustled with playing children. Girls were screaming, swinging, and singing. Boys were jumping, bumping, and thumping. Children were crawling, falling, brawling, and sprawling everywhere.

Mary mounted the slide and zipped down, banging her bottom in the dirt. The impact stunned her for a moment, then picking herself up, she saw a shy, black-eyed girl smiling at her.

"Would you jump rope with me?" asked the girl.

"I guess so. What's your name?"

"Lola," she replied. "Lola Nola Mazola."

They jumped rope for a long time. Then they climbed the jungle-gym and scrambled over the horizontal bars.

Then Lola Nola Mazola had to leave.

As afternoon faded into twilight, Mary decided on a final trip down the slide. Climbing the steps, she found a dirty-faced girl awaiting her at the top. The girl eyed her with scorn.

"I s'pose you wanna go down the slide," said the girl. "I s'pose that's just what you want to do. Well, you can't. I'm not gonna let you."

The holes in her nose flared a little. Then she continued, "I have to give permission. I'm Princess of the Playground, and no one can slide without paying the tax."

"What's the tax?"

"One twenty-five cent quarter," snarled the girl.

"A quarter!" cried Mary. "A quarter to use this slide! This isn't your slide! This . . . this is a free park!! This is a public slide!! I use it whenever I want to."

3

"No way!" sneered the girl. "I'm the Playground Princess, and you can't go down this slide without permission. You gotta pay the tax."

Mary tried to say something clever, but nothing came from her mouth except, "I'm not paying your stupid tax!" The girl laughed.

"Get out of my way!" shouted Mary.

"Make me!"

Mary grabbed the girl's arm, trying to push her aside. But she had to hold the ladder with one hand. The other girl, propped atop the slide, fought dirty. She slapped and flapped and clapped. She bit and spit and hit. She shoved Mary with her foot, sending her plummeting backward through the air. Mary fell with a thud into the sand. For a moment she couldn't move. Her lungs were stunned! Then she gulped big sobs, gasping for air.

Husky hands and strong arms suddenly slid under her. Her father lifted her to himself and held her tightly. Talking gently, he walked to the park bench and wiped her face with a wet handkerchief. Then he inspected her for damage.

There wasn't any. At least, no serious damage. Mary watched the "Princess" being hauled home by an angry grown-up. Then Mary and her dad walked to the ice cream shop.

As they sipped their Razzleberry milk shakes, Mary asked her father, "Why are some people so mean?"

He thought a moment before answering. "We all have meanness in our hearts, Mary," he explained. "Jesus Christ is the only one who can help us with it. Perhaps the Princess of the Playground doesn't know about Him yet."

Mary played with her straw, thinking about her dad's words.

"Then I guess we'll just have to tell her about Him," she finally said.

"Yes," replied her father. "I guess we will."

Then Mary slurped her milk shake, and they walked home.

Mary learned some things during her adventures in the park. Take a few moments to answer these questions, and see if you can make some similar discoveries.

1. Who liked Mary and wanted to play with her and why?

_____

_____

2. Who disliked her and why?

_____

_____

3. Who loved Mary and why?

_____

_____

4. How can you tell he loved her?

_____

_____

5. Name some people who love you.

_____

_____

6. How does it feel to be loved?

_____

_____

7. According to **John 3:16**, who loves you more than anyone else?

_____

_____

8. Though God loves us with unfailing love, we don't always love Him as we should. What did Mary's father tell her we all have in our hearts?

_____

_____

9. What word does the Bible sometimes use to describe our *meanness*? _____

Romans 3:23: . . . for all have _____ned and fall short of the glory of God.

10. Draw a picture of something that happened in the story that displeased God.

11. Can you name things you have done that have been displeasing to God?

_____

_____

12. Should the girl who pushed Mary from the top of the sliding board be punished? Why or why not?

YES   NO

_____

_____

13. Disobedience and sin must be punished, and since everyone in the world has sinned against God, everyone deserves to be punished. What is the penalty for sin? _____
Romans 6:23: "For the wages (penalty) of sin is _____."

14. But the Bible also teaches that, although God must punish sin, He wants to forgive us. He sent someone else to take our penalty. **Romans 5:8** says: "But God demonstrates His own love for us in this: While we were still sinners, _____ for us."

REMEMBER THIS:
We all have meanness—sin—in our lives.
Sin must be punished, but God loves us
and sent Christ to die for us.
—Mary Motley

2. HERMAN HACKLER'S HORRIBLE DAY

Herman Hackler was having a horrible day. His dad had promised to take him fishing, but just as they were packing their gear, the phone rang.

"Is Dr. Hackler there?" asked the nurse. Herman wanted to lie. He knew the call meant that his father, a busy doctor, was needed at the hospital. "Just a minute," he sighed. He heard his dad's end of the conversation: "Yes . . . Yes . . . How many? I'm on my way."

With a gloomy smile, Dr. Hackler glanced at his son. "Sorry, pal. There's been a wreck. They need me in the emergency room."

As the door slammed, Herman flopped across the sofa like a weary warrior who had just lost a battle. His chin quivered.

"You need something to do," suggested his mom. "Why don't you rake the leaves. Your father will never get around to it." Herman hated raking leaves. But his mom insisted, and he found the rake in the garage. He dragged it across the ground.

He had just made his first little pile when the hornet stung him. He had squeezed it in the joint of his arm as he pulled the rake toward him. It jabbed his skin like an ice pick. It throbbed and burned. Then it ached and itched.

But it didn't get him out of raking the lawn. By noon, he had fifteen little piles of leaves.

Herman's mother served him a cheese sandwich for lunch. He hated cheese sandwiches. They always gummed up in his mouth, but he nibbled at it, ate the chips, and drank his cola. After stuffing his leaves into bags, he slung his bat over his shoulder and walked down the street. At the end of the block, a group of older guys was playing baseball in a vacant field. Herman was a good player, but he was only ten. These guys were in junior high, but they weren't very good. Herman was better, and he knew it. He walked over to the third baseman.

"Can I play?" he asked.

"Scram, kid!"

"I want to play, and I'm good," Herman persisted.

"Get outta my way, kid. We got a game goin' on here."

"Why can't I play? I'm a better player than you are any day!"

"I said beat it, boy!"

Just then the batter blasted the ball toward the third baseman who lurched for the catch. He stumbled over Herman, and both of them tumbled into the dirt. The catch was lost, and the player was furious.

"Now look what you've done!" he screamed at Herman. "Just look what you've done! Get outta here, kid, before I kick you all the way home!" Then turning to the other players, he shouted, "It was the lousy kid's fault."

Herman's face reddened and, for the second time that day, his chin quivered. He stormed away, dragging his bat behind him. He felt humiliated.

The more he thought about it, the angrier he became. He resented his dad for being a doctor and his mom for serving cheese sandwiches. He was mad at the trees for shedding leaves and at hornets for stinging. Most of all, his blood boiled over the third baseman.

Every step pounded the anger deeper into his heart—like a hammer driving nails into cement. He wiped his nose, and thought about that third baseman. He closed his eyes and thought about being called a "lousy kid." His chin quivered again. Then the fury inside him exploded. He flung his bat to the sidewalk. He threw down his glove. Taking deliberate aim, he sent his baseball toward Mrs. Von Roddersnot's kitchen window.

It was a direct hit.

"I told them I was a good player," he mumbled to himself, and trudged home. His dad was waiting for him in the driveway, and Herman suddenly felt sick.

"Jeannette Von Roddersnot just called. Said you threw your baseball through her kitchen window. Said you did it deliberately."

Herman wasn't a cry-baby, but all the emotion of the day welled up inside him. He sat on the ground and tears rolled down his cheeks. He blew his nose.

His dad sprawled beside him on the grass, and Herman told him all about his horrible day. They talked together for a long time. Dr. Hackler wasn't angry. He listened carefully and seemed to understand. But in the end, he told Herman that he had to confess to Mrs. Von Roddersnot that he had broken her window. He also had to pay for the repairs.

They plodded down the street. Herman rang the doorbell and heard footsteps within the house. Opening the door, Mrs. Von Roddersnot peered at Herman through horned glasses.

"Yes?" she snarled.

"I broke your window, Mrs. Von Roddersnot, and I'm very sorry. I'd like to know how I can make it up to you."

"Well," she snapped, "I saw you do it on purpose."

"I was mad," replied Herman. "But not at you. I was angry with . . . Well, I was just angry and I wanted to hit something. I'm sorry."

"It will cost thirty-eight dollars and twenty-nine cents to repair. I've already called about it."

Herman's heart raced. "I don't have that much money," he stammered. "I only have twelve dollars and ninety-nine cents."

"That isn't enough. The bill is exactly thirty-eight dollars and twenty-nine cents. Exactly."

As Herman groped for words, he felt a hand on his shoulder. He turned, and his dad handed him something. Two twenty-dollar bills. He understood.

"Here," he said, handing them to the lady. "Keep the change." Without a word, she took the money, snorted, and closed the door.

As they walked home, Herman and his dad were quiet. But as they entered the house, Dr. Hackler said, "Herman, Old Wally owns a fishing cabin on Juniper Lake. He isn't using it tonight and the weather's going to be perfect tomorrow. Wanna go?"

"Tonight?"

"Tonight!" grinned his dad.

Herman grabbed his fishing pole while his father loaded the car and his mother packed them a supper of chips, colas—and grilled cheese sandwiches.

Have you ever had a bad day like Herman's? Everyone finds some days harder than others. Here are some questions to help today be a good day for you.

1. Should Herman have thrown his ball through the neighbor's window?

   YES   ~~NO~~

2. Herman had to admit his wrongdoing to two people—his dad, and who else?

   _____

3. What was the penalty for his wrong action?

   _____

   _____

4. Could he pay the cost?

   YES   ~~NO~~

5. Who paid it for him? (Circle the correct answer)

   Herman   Mrs. Von Roddersnot   God   ~~His dad~~   Mary Motley

6. We have sinned against God. Remember what **Romans 3:23** says? "_____ have sinned." The penalty for our sins is _____ (**Romans 6:23**). "But God demonstrated His love for us in this: While we were still sinners, _____ died for us" (**Romans 5:8**).

   Jesus loved us and paid our penalty for the meanness in our hearts — just like Dr. Hackler paid the penalty Herman couldn't afford. Christ paid this penalty by dying on the cross and rising from the dead. Read aloud this description of Jesus' death and resurrection. It comes from **Luke 23 and 24.**

   > When they came to the place called the Skull, there they crucified Him, along with the criminals—one on His right, the other on His left. Jesus said, "Father, forgive them, for they do not know what they are doing." And they divided up His clothes. The people stood

watching, and the rulers sneered at Him. They said, "He saved others; let Him save Himself if He is the Christ of God, the Chosen One."

The soldiers also came up and mocked Him. One of the criminals who hung there hurled insults at Him: "Aren't you the Christ? Save yourself and us!" But the other criminal rebuked him. "Don't you fear God," he said, "since you are under the same sentence? We are punished justly, for we are getting what our deeds deserve. But this man has done nothing wrong."

Then he said, "Jesus, remember me when you come into your kingdom." Jesus answered him, "I tell you the truth, today you will be with me in paradise."

It was now about the sixth hour, and darkness came over the whole land until the ninth hour, for the sun stopped shining. Jesus called out with a loud voice, "Father, into Your hands I commit My spirit." When He had said this, He breathed His last.

On the first day of the week, very early in the morning, the women took the spices they had prepared and went to the tomb. They found the stone rolled away from the tomb, but when they entered, they could not find the body of the Lord Jesus. While they were wondering about this, suddenly two men in clothes that gleamed like lightning stood beside them. In their fright the women bowed down with their faces to the ground, but the men said to them, "Why do you look for the living among the dead? He is not here; He has risen!"

Because of what Jesus did for us, We can ask Him to forgive our sins. We can ask Him to be our Best Friend and to help us please Him. That's the meaning of **Romans 10:13:** "Everyone who calls on the name of the Lord will be saved." When we do that, Jesus becomes our Savior. The word "Savior" means "One who saves us." He saves us from sin and death.

Does that mean we'll never die? Yes! Our bodies may die and be buried, but our souls go to heaven. Someday our bodies will rise from the grave just like Jesus' body did on Easter Sunday. We'll live forever with Him!

Would you like to ask Jesus to forgive your sins and become your Savior? Would you like to know that you're going to live forever? If so, bow your head and talk to Him. Pray this prayer, or one like it:

Dear God,
I know that I've disobeyed You. I admit that I have meanness inside me. I'm sorry for the bad things I've done. I ask You to forgive me, I want You to become my Best Friend. I invite Jesus Christ to be my Savior. Please help me live in a way that pleases you. I pray this in Jesus' name.
Amen.

Date: _____
Signed:_____

If you have already prayed a prayer like this, receiving Christ as your Savior, finish this paragraph:

I have already asked Christ to forgive my sin. I received Him as
my Savior on or about _____ (date).
Signed:_____

MEMORIZE THIS VERSE

"For God so loved the world that He gave His one and only Son, that whoever believes in Him shall not perish but have eternal life." –John 3:16

PART 2:
SHOWING

3. THE NEXT STEP

"And the winner is . . ."

Miss Drizzle pulled the name from the sealed envelope, reading it to herself.

Milly's heart was galloping. She had entered the *Mashville Gazette's* young authors' contest with a story called *Mary's Stage Fright.* The story was about her younger sister's ordeal at a school play. It had been chosen the best among all seventh-grade entries in her school. Now she was about to learn if it had won the city-wide competition. This year's winner would have the honor of meeting a former president of the United States whose presence on the platform seemed to electrify the crowd.

"And the winner is . . . MILLY MOTLEY!"

The audience roared, and Milly squealed as she leaped from her seat toward the platform. She mounted the steps and smiled at Miss Drizzle. She accepted her blue ribbon and smiled at the crowd. Then Milly walked over to the former president.

Offering his hand, he said, "Congratulations, Milly."

Then Milly froze, suddenly realizing how her little sister must have felt during her play. She shivered and quivered. She fluttered and shuttered and muttered and stuttered, "Th . . . Thank you, Mr. Present. I mean, Mr. Resident . . . I mean, Sir President, Mister." A camera flashed in their faces, then Milly returned to her seat.

The next morning her best friend, Tessie, called with exciting news. "Milly, have you seen the paper? Your picture with the president is right in the middle of page one!"

Hanging up the phone, Milly slipped to her room and removed a little box from her dresser. She opened it carefully and took out several dollars. Shoving them into her pocket, she hopped downstairs.

"I'm going to the corner market," she yelled. She ran down the street to Melody Market, found the newspaper rack, and loaded her arms with twenty copies of the *Mashville Gazette!*

Old Wally grinned as she approached his register. He was a grandfatherly man—tall and baldish, with gray stubble on his cheeks. Milly enjoyed talking with him, but she always spoke loudly for Wally had grown hard of hearing.

"What'er you goin' do with them papers?" he asked.

"I'm buying them to send to people."

"You're tryin' to mend the steeple?" Wally cried. "What happened to it?"

"Nothing. I said I want to put these papers in the mail!"

"It was hail! Well, by crickedy, I remember a hailstorm that struck our farm when I'ze a boy. Punched holes in our tin roof. And them hailstones—they fell into my lil' bedroom like marbles from heaven. The next mornin' when I got outta bed, I stepped on 'em and rolled right out the front door in my underwear."

"We didn't have a storm," snickered Milly. "I won the writer's contest, and my picture's on page one of the *Gazette.*"

"Jeannette? Jeannette Von Roddersnot?" asked Wally. "Was she caught 'n the hail storm? I hope she didn't roll out the door like I did!"

"Wally," said Milly, unfolding the paper. "Look here."

The old man reached in his shirt pocket for his glasses. As he saw Milly's picture, his eyes sparkled.

"Well, lookie there! My lil' Milly with a former pres'dent of the USA. Just look a' that, will you! In all my born days, I never met a pres'dent."

He studied the picture some more, then added, "If I'ze you, I'd send this here picture to my kin folk."

"That's what I'm doing. I'm going to send copies to all my relatives. That's why I'm buying these papers this morning."

Wally looked up with concern. "A warning, you say? It's goin' a' hail again, is it?"

Milly laughed as she made her purchase, tucked the papers under her arm, and headed for the door. But as she left, she heard old Wally chuckling to himself:

"So Jeannette Von Roddersnot got caught in the hailstorm, did she? Well, by crickedy, I do declare—I'd like to have seen that!"

Sooner or later most of us meet a famous person, and we usually enjoy talking about it later. Think about Milly's experience and answer the following questions.

1. Why did Milly want to send copies of the *Mashville Gazette* to her friends and relatives?

   _____

   _____

2. If you could meet anyone in the world, who would you choose?

   _____

   _____

3. Would you want to tell someone else about it? _____

4. Meeting Christ is even better than meeting the president of the United States. Jesus is the most famous person in history, and meeting Him is far better than meeting anyone else. We "meet" Christ when we ask Him to be our Savior and Best Friend. When that happens, we want to share our experience with others. Your picture may not be in the newspaper, but others can still learn of your decision. Think of some ways you can let others know of your new relationship with Christ.

   _____

   _____

One of the best ways to show others you've become a Christian is by being baptized. What is baptism? Why are people baptized? What happens when you are baptized? Look up the following verses to find out.

5. Read **Matthew 3:13–16**

   Describe below what is going on in this Scripture.

   _____

   _____

6. Read **Acts 2:40–41**

Peter told these people about Jesus, inviting them to receive Him as Savior. Some of them accepted his message and became Christians. What did they do next?

A. They jumped up and down.

B. They were baptized.

C. They memorized the Twenty-Third Psalm.

7. Read **Acts 8:36–39**

Philip told his friend about the Lord Jesus as they rode together in a chariot. The man received Jesus as his Savior. Draw a picture of what happened next.

8. What happens when I'm baptized?

Everyone in the New Testament who received Jesus was baptized. You can be, too. What happens when you are baptized? In some churches, you and the pastor step into a small pool of water. He holds your back and chest, slowly lowering you into the water. Then he quickly lifts you out. It's as simple as that, and you can hold your nose if you wish. It isn't frightening, but it's very important.

9. What does being baptized mean?

When Jesus died on the cross, He died in an **up**right position. When they buried Him, they laid him **down** on a stone slab in the tomb. When He rose from the dead, He stood **up** again.

UP   **UP**

DOWN

When the pastor baptizes you, you first stand **up** straight in the water. Then you're lowered **down** into the water. Then you come **up** again. Just like Jesus.

UP   **UP**

DOWN

It shows everyone that you have decided to follow the One who died, was buried, and rose again for you. You are following the example of Christ. If you have accepted Him as Savior, He wants you to share that good news by being baptized. Call your church office, and ask to meet with a pastor or worker. He or she will explain your church's baptismal requirements and procedures. When the time comes for your baptism, ask a church worker or friend to take a picture of it for the box on the next page. Your pastor can sign and date the accompanying certificate.

MEMORIZE THIS VERSE

We were therefore buried with Him through baptism into death in order that, just as Christ was raised from the dead through the glory of the Father, we too may live a new life.
–Romans 6:4

Certificate of Baptism

This is to certify that

_____

having professed faith in Jesus Christ
was baptized in the name of
the Father,
the Son,
and the Holy Spirit
on

_____

at

_____

by

_____

Minister

_____

Witness
(Picture)

PART 3: GROWING

G Go to Church

R Read Your Bible and Pray

O Obey

W Witness

4. NOW WHAT?

One day when Mary and her new friend, Lola Nola Mazola, were reading a puzzle book, they came across the following quiz. "Some of these people," it said, "are wise. Put a **W** beside them and put a **F** beside the foolish ones." The two girls guessed correctly every time. See if you can, too.

_____**MARK CLARK** was an artist. His studio was full of paintings, none of them finished. Every time he began a picture, he lost interest in it. He had 689 half-done paintings.

_____**JENNY FINNEY** started cleaning her room. It was a hard job and she became tired. She felt like giving up. But she kept at it until everything was in its place.

_____**RAY GRAY** was quarterback for his football team. On the opening play, he tossed the ball to the tailback, yawned, and walked off the field.

_____**BART HART** decided to earn $32 for a fishing pole. He washed cars, raked leaves, walked dogs, and swept porches. He earned $12, and gave up the project. He thought the work was too hard.

_____**NANCY CLANCY** had tons of homework. She opened her spelling book, but she didn't feel like doing her assignment. She opened her English book, but the first question was too hard to think about. She opened her reading book, but she had forgotten what page to read. So she closed her books and watched television.

_____**JERRY BERRY** determined to run a mile with his dad. After only one block, his lungs gasped for air. His side split with pain. The next day he ran a block and a half before quitting. Saturday he went three blocks. Every day he went a little further. Exactly one month later, he finished his mile.

What was the difference between the wise and the foolish people?

_____

_____

Asking Jesus to be your Savior is only the beginning. Jesus told a story in **Matthew 13** that warned His followers to remain faithful. Some people, He said, hear the Savior's message and appear to receive it. But they become so busy with other things they forget Christ. Others, finding the Christian life too hard, give up. Still others don't really understand what they must do to grow.

But real Christians stay true to Christ. They keep on growing like golden stalks of wheat.

In **Luke 2:52** Jesus Christ is described as a boy who grew from a baby to become a strong, healthy young man. He matured, according to Luke, in four different ways. Study the verse, then finish the chart below:

Jesus Grew . . .

| Mentally | Physically | Spiritually | Socially |

"Jesus grew in _____ and _____ and in favor with_____ and _____."
   —Luke 2:52

28

How can you grow spiritually like Jesus did? The secret is found in that very word: **GROW!** We'll see how in coming lessons, but first, complete this project to help you memorize an important verse of Scripture.

- Locate an old flower pot, buy an inexpensive one at the store, or punch some holes in the bottom of a tin can.
- Fill it with potting soil.
- Plant some flower seeds in it, or transplant a green plant into the dirt.
- Cut out the following verse, fold it over the top of a soda straw, making a sign. Then stick it in the pot.
- Every time you water your plant, say the verse aloud until it's memorized.

MEMORIZE THIS VERSE

"But grow in the grace and knowledge of our Lord and Savior Jesus Christ. To Him be glory both now and forever! Amen." –2 Peter 3:18

5. GO TO CHURCH!

They all loved pizza, but Mary and her sisters, Milly and Molly, also liked spaghetti. Only Molly ate lobster tails, but all three sometimes ate hot dogs. Milly liked hamburgers but without the bun.

They all enjoyed vacations, but Milly preferred hotels to camping in the woods.

Molly liked horses but not boys (she was eleven). Milly liked boys but not horses (she was thirteen). And Mary? Well, Mary liked dogs and horses; she wasn't sure about boys yet.

All three sisters were different with their own special tastes. But there was one thing they all enjoyed: They loved *going to church each Sunday!*

They knew that the church isn't really a building. It's a group of people who have asked Jesus Christ to be their Savior. These people love each other, and they think of each other as brothers and sisters. They meet together to worship God and to learn more about Him.

One Sunday Milly, Molly, and Mary attended a special class that studied the following questions about the church. Study along with them, and see if you can learn as much as they did:

1. What day of the week did the early Christians set aside for worship? _____
   (Look up **John 20:1, 19, 26; Acts 20:7**)

2. What do we call this day? _____

3. What did the Christians in the Bible call this day? _____
   (Look up **Revelation 1:10**)

4. What did they do as they met together? _____
   (Look up **Acts 2:42, 46–47; 17:11**)

31

5. "Breaking bread" was a custom among New Testament Christians that combined an evening meal with the observance of the Lord's Supper. The Lord's Supper is a ceremony in which Christians eat a small piece of bread and drink a swallow of juice. It has a special meaning.

Read **Luke 22:19-20**

What does the bread stand for? _____

What does the cup of juice represent? _____

The bread and the juice are symbols of the body and blood of Jesus Christ. A symbol is a picture or object that stands for something else. For example, below are some symbols, and, on the right, the things they stand for. Draw lines matching the items together.

Stack of money

Symbol of the United States

Building of American Forestry Service

December 25 on a calendar

Drugstore

Bottle labeled "Poison"

Athletic Events

Valentines Day

In the same way, the bread and the juice of the Lord's Supper are symbols of the body and blood of Christ. When we eat the bread and drink the juice, it helps us remember that Jesus died on the cross for us. It reminds us that He has saved us from eternal death. That's why He said in **Luke 22:19**: "Do this in _____ of Me."

6. See if you can find in this word search seven things we do at church:

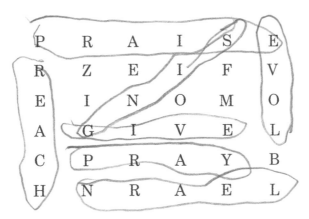

7. Have you ever fallen asleep in church? **Acts 20:7–12** describes an evening church service in the days of the apostle Paul. Read about it, then draw a picture of an unusual thing that happened that night.

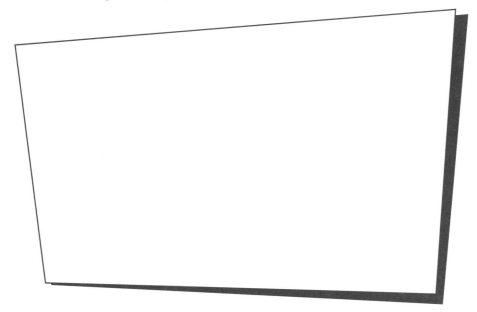

MEMORIZE THIS VERSE

"Let us not give up meeting together, as some are in the habit of doing, but let us encourage one another—and all the more as you see the Day approaching." –Hebrews 10:25

Word Search Answers on page 56

6. READ YOUR BIBLE AND PRAY!

"Dad, why do you enjoy being a Christian so much?" Molly asked.

"The most exciting thing about being a Christian," he replied, "is talking with God each day. Though He guides the stars and guards the world, He still has time to talk with you and me."

"But how can I talk with God? I can't call Him on the telephone, can I?"

"No," laughed her father. "When we talk *with* someone, we both *listen* to them and *speak* to them. We listen to God by reading His Word, the Bible, and we speak to Him when we pray."

Molly wanted to learn more about Bible study and prayer, so she and her father looked up the following verses. Why don't you study along with them.

BIBLE STUDY

1. When did Timothy begin learning the Bible? (Look up **2 Timothy 3:14–16**)

_____

_____

2. What did the people in the town of Berea do each day? (Look up **Acts 17:11**)

_____

_____

3. What can keep us from sinning against God? (Look up **Psalm 119:11**)

_____

_____

The Bible is a big book made up of sixty-six smaller books, beginning with Genesis and ending with Revelation. The first thirty-nine books are called the ***Old Testament,*** and they tell us about things that happened before Jesus was born.

The final twenty-seven books are called the *New Testament.* The New Testament begins with four books called the Gospels. The four Gospels tell us the story of the life of Jesus Christ, as written by Matthew, Mark, Luke, and John. The next book, Acts, tells us about the early days of the church. The rest of the New Testament is letters that church leaders like Paul wrote to the congregations of New Testament times.

Old Testament

39 books

History—Poetry—Prophecy

New Testament

27 books

Gospels—Acts—Letters

PRAYER

1. What did Jesus tell us to do when we pray? (Find the answer in **Matthew 6:6**)

_____

_____

2. What does the Lord promise to do when we pray according to His will? (Study **1 John 5:14-15**)

_____

_____

What does it really mean to pray? It means that we talk to God, either aloud or silently, just as we would talk to another person. We should begin by **rejoicing**—praising Him for being so good to us and thanking Him for specific things He has done for us. Then we ask Him to forgive us for wrong things we've done. We tell Him we're sorry, asking Him to help us improve our behavior or attitudes. That is called **repenting**. Then, we tell Him our **requests**—praying for our needs and for the needs of others. To develop a good prayer habit, just remember those three Rs:

Rejoice Repent Request

Think back over the things you've just read. Then take this little quiz. See how many answers you can complete correctly.

1. How many books are in the Bible?

    A. 2   B. 66   C. 4,739,872   D. 0

2. Who studied their Bibles every day?

    A. The four Gospels   C. The Chicago Bulls

    B. Lola Nola Mazola   D. The people of Berea

3. What are the 3 R's of prayer?

    R_____ **R**_____ & **R**_____

4. Which has more books—the Old Testament or the New Testament? (Circle the right one)

5. The first book of the Bible is

    A. Genesis

    B. Matthew

    C. Revelation

    D. John 3:16

6. Who told us to go into our rooms, close the door, and pray?

_____

_____

7. When we tell God we're sorry for our sins and ask Him to help us improve, we are:

    A. Reading our Bibles

    B. Sipping Razzleberry Milkshakes

    C. Rejoicing

    D. Repenting

8. The Gospels are the first four books of the New Testament, and they tell us the story of:
   A. John
   B. Jesus
   C. Old Wally

9. The promise that God will answer our prayers when we pray them according to His will is found in:
   A. the gospel of John
   B. 1 John
   C. 2 John
   D. 3 John
   E. The *Mashville Gazette*

10. Prayer is _____

Every Christian should have a regular time and place to talk with God, spending a few minutes each day reading His Word and praying. On the next page is a one-week project to help you begin your daily habit of meeting with God. When would be a good time each day for you to talk with the Lord?

ONE FULL WEEK OF TALKING WITH GOD

The next page will help you begin a habit of reading the Bible and praying each day. Here are seven passages to read from the gospel of John, one for each day of the week. Read the verses and answer the questions. Then talk to the Lord, telling Him anything you'd like. He wants to listen. On a separate sheet of paper begin a prayer list to remind you of the items you want to pray about each day.

Day 1: John 3:1-16

What does God give to those who believe in His Son (verse 16)?

_____

Day 2: John 6:1-15

Who had something that Jesus could use (verse 9)?

_____

What did Jesus do with it?

_____

Day 3: John 6:16-21

How did Jesus save the disciples from drowning?

_____

Day 4: John 10:10-15

If Jesus is the good shepherd, what are we?

_____

Day 5: John 19:16-30

What happened to Jesus?

_____

Day 6: John 20:1-9

What was empty? Why?

_____

Day 7: John 20:24-31

What did Thomas discover?

_____

7. OBEY!

"You're stupid!"

Molly spit out the words before slamming the back door. She shook with anger.

"Molly! Who were you screaming at?" said her mother with alarm. "We don't ever call people *stupid!*"

"I wasn't talking to a person. I was shouting at Mr. Muscle. He ran off again. He dug under the fence, and before I could stop him, he was gone."

"Oh!"

"When I yelled for him, he looked at me a moment, then turned and took off."

"Where was he going?"

"How should I know! I guess he's just following his toes."

"You mean, 'he's following his nose.' But I can hardly believe that a Great Dane like Mr. Muscle could crawl under the fence."

"Well, he did, Mom. And when I yelled at him, he didn't obey."

"It makes you mad, doesn't it."

"Makes me furious," replied Molly, "and scared. I'm afraid he'll be hit by a car or thrown in the pound."

"I'm afraid he'll wander onto Mrs. Von Roddersnot's front yard. She would probably shoot him, thinking he was a monster."

"Well, it would be his own fault," said Molly.

"Well, try to relax, Molly. He's run off before and has always come back in a few minutes. He'll probably ramble home after while."

"Yeah," said Molly. "He'll be back, all right—just in time for supper."

1. Why did Molly want Mr. Muscle to obey her?

_____

_____

_____

_____

_____

_____

2. Look up the word *obey* in a dictionary. What does it mean?

_____

_____

_____

_____

_____

_____

Jesus often spoke of the importance of obedience. Finish these verses:

John 14:15: "If you love me, you will _____ what I command."

John 14:21: "Whoever has my commands and obeys them, he is the one

who _____ me."

John 14:23: "If anyone _____ me, he will _____ my teaching."

John 14:24: "He who does not love me will not _____ my teaching."

Jesus wants us to obey His rules in the Bible, so that we'll be safe and happy. Just as Molly was displeased with Mr. Muscle, and frightened for him, the Lord Jesus is displeased with us when we disobey, because He knows that disobedience hurts us. But as we discover and obey His commands in the Scripture, He blesses us with joy and happiness. This crossword puzzle will help you find some of God's wonderful commands.

ACROSS

1. According to **Colossians 3:20**, a child should obey his or her "ma" and "___."

3. Mary Motley's initials

8. **Colossians 3:13** says, "Forgive _____ the Lord forgave you."

9. According to **Colossians 3:20**, when we obey our parents we _____ the Lord.

12. **Colossians 3:16** tells us to "_____ psalms, hymns, and spiritual songs . . ."

13. The number of people who would be in church if no one came.

14. Jesus told us to enter the narrow _____.**(Matthew 7:13)**

16. The first woman **(Genesis 3:20)**

17. We should _____ every kind of evil. **(1 Thessalonians 5:22)**

19. Opposite of # 30 down

20. We should live for the glory of God whether "in word or in _____."
    (Colossians 3:17)

22. The angels at the empty tomb of Christ told the women to go and _____ the disciples that Jesus had risen from the grave **(Matthew 28:7)**

24. We must _____ ourselves of anger, rage, malice, slander and filthy language.**(Colossians 3:8)**

25. Paul told Archippus: "_____ to it that you complete the work!"
    (Colossians 4:17)

28. "Let the _____ of Christ rule in your hearts . . ."**(Colossians 3:15)**

29. We must not use filthy _____ **(Colossians 3:8)**

32. The Colossians lived in the city of Colosse. What kind of book would you look in to find its location on a map?

DOWN

1. **Colossians 3:20** tells children to obey their _Parents_.

2. Just ___AS___ you received Christ Jesus as Lord, continue to live in Him . . . **(Colossians 2:6)**

3. The opposite of "you."

4. These men followed the star to the Christ-child. **(Matthew 2:1)**

5. "_____ the peace of Christ rule in your hearts." **(Colossians 3:15)**

6. Christ forgave _____ all our sins. **(Colossians 2:13)**

7. According to **Colossians 3:8**, we must rid ourselves of this.

9. **Colossians 4:2-3** tells us that we should _____ for others.

10. **Colossians 3:14** tells us that we should _____ others.

11. These people did not believe Jesus. **(Matthew 22:23)**

13. **Romans 12:11** tells us that we should never lack this.

15. People who know Christ live for _____.

18. If we obey **Colossians 3:15**, we will not be grumpy like _____ the Grouch.

21. According to **1 Timothy 4:15**, when it comes to obedience, we should be _____, so that everyone can see our progress.

23. According to **Colossians 3:9**, we aren't to do this.

26. In **Colossians 3:12**, we are called "God's chosen people, _____ . . ."

27. The man who wrote Colossians. **(Colossians 1:1)**

30. According to **Titus 3:1-2**, this is what we should say when a friend tempts us to disobey.

31. What Jesus told us to do with the gospel. **(Matthew 28:19)**

OBEY!
CROSSWORD PUZZLE

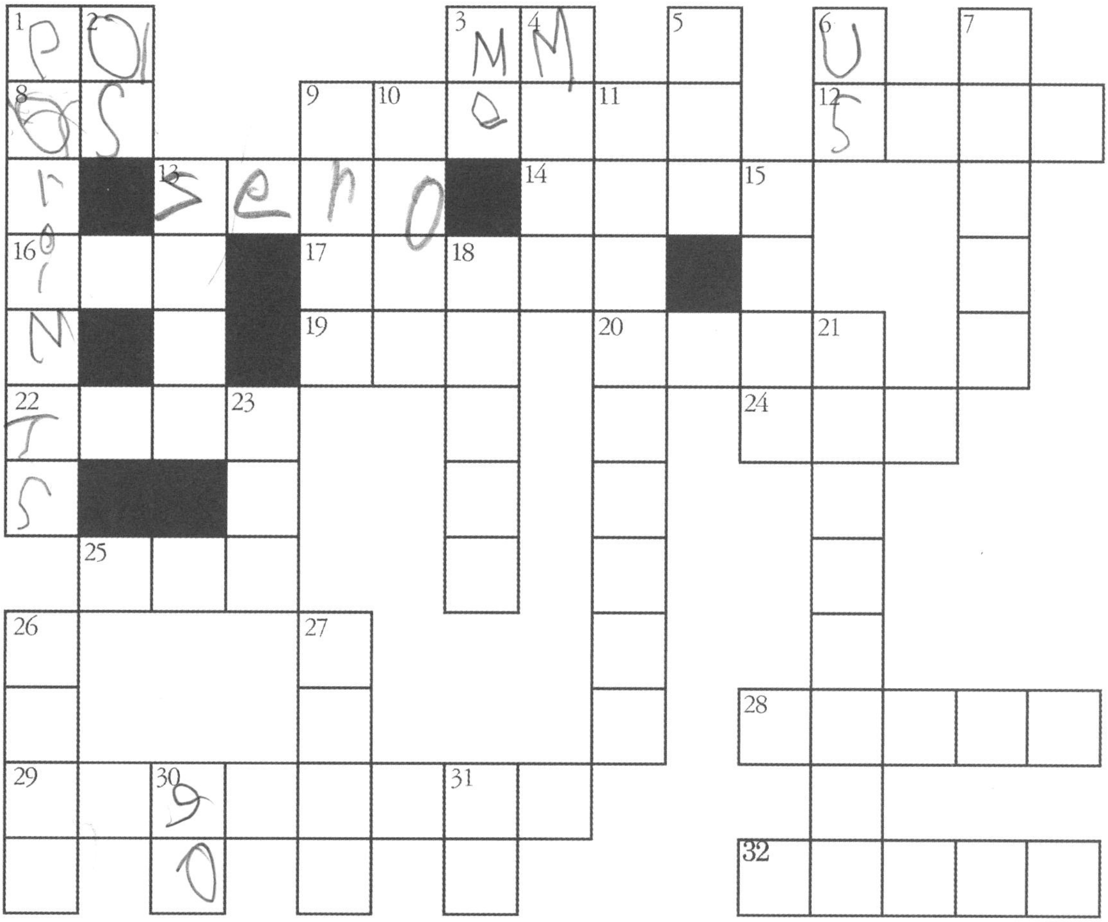

Obey Crossword Answers on page 56

8. THE WITNESS

At high noon on July 19, Herman Hackler witnessed a wreck. He was sitting under a maple tree near his house, dripping with sweat. He had just finished a sizzling baseball game on the corner lot, and his mom had given him a tall glass of lemonade. Sipping his drink, he watched the squirrels romp in the neighbor's trees.

Just then a delivery truck, rumbling down the street, jerked and swerved. Herman's eyes shot toward it. He heard brakes screech, tires slide, and horns blare! As he watched, the truck crashed into the rear fender of a car that had just backed out of a driveway. Herman's chin quivered.

The car and driveway belonged to Jeannette Von Roddersnot! She had roared from her driveway without even looking.

Mrs. Von Roddersnot, unhurt, vaulted from her vehicle, saw her crumpled fender, and eyed the truck driver with disgust.

"Look what you have done to my automobile," she snapped. "You will surely pay for this."

"It wasn't my fault, lady," declared the truck driver. "You backed right in front of me."

"Well, it wouldn't have happened if you had been paying attention," she snorted. "This street is no place for trucks anyway."

When the squad car arrived, a police officer walked over to Herman. "Did you witness the accident, son?"

"Well, I saw what happened if that's what you mean."

"That's exactly what I mean. A *witness* is someone who knows something, and who tells exactly what he knows. Can you tell me exactly what you know about the wreck?"

Herman told the policeman exactly what he had seen. The officer filed the report, and guess who was charged with careless driving? Guess who had to pay for the repairs to the vehicles?

It amounted to a good deal more than $38.29.

Do you realize that you can be a witness, too? Think about it. In this story:

1. A witness is someone who . . .

    A. had an automobile accident

    B. plays baseball

    C. knows something important, and tells it

    D. sits under a tree, sipping lemonade

2. Jesus said: "You will be my _____ " (look up **Acts 1:8**). What do you think He meant by that?

    _____

    _____

3. Here are some ways you can be a witness for Christ. Can you add to it?

    A. Invite someone to Sunday school

    B. Tell a friend that Jesus loves them

    C. Write to friends, telling them that you've asked Jesus to be your Savior

    D. Give a friend a copy of this book

    E. _____

    F. _____

    G. _____

    H. _____

4. List the names of three people you can pray for who need Christ.

    _____

    _____

    _____

On the next page is the issue of the *Mashville Gazette,* published on the day of Mrs. Von Roddersnot's accident. Use your imagination to finish the headline and picture.

9. GERMS, JOAN, AND JOHN 3:16

Mary Motley sneezed. It was her twenty-third sneeze that morning. Once again, it caught her off guard, and she sprayed the room with billions of germs.

"Mary!" cried her mother. "I've told you a hundred times to cover your mouth!" But Mrs. Motley's frown faded into concern as she saw Mary's red eyes and wet forehead.

"Your cold is getting worse, isn't it?" she asked. "I'll call Dr. Hackler's office for an appointment this afternoon."

Fear flickered on Mary's face. "Will he give me a shot?" she asked. Her mother just shrugged and reached for the phone.

That afternoon as Mary entered the clinic, she noticed a tattered girl sitting alone on a bench in the corner. Her leg rested in a heavy cast, and a pair of crutches lay beside her. She seemed sad.

"I've seen that girl before," thought Mary. "Where have I met her? Yes, of course! She's the Princess of the Playground."

"Mom," whispered Mary. "See that girl in the corner? She's the girl who . . . who . . . ACH . . . **ACHOOOO!"**

A shower of wet germs drenched the air.

"Mary Motley!" cried her mom. "Why can't you cover your mouth? I feel like I'm in a rain forest. You're going to make us all sick!"

Before Mary could wipe her nose and apologize, a white-starched nurse came to the door.

"Mary Motley. This way please. Down the hall. Third door on the right. Dr. Hackler will see you shortly. Put this under your tongue." The nurse shoved a cold thermometer in her mouth, and Mary did as told. A few minutes later Dr. Hackler entered the room.

"Well, well, Mary!" he bellowed. "Have a cold, have we? My Herman's sick, too. Caught cold on a fishing trip. I gave him a shot yesterday."

Mary wanted to explain that she felt fine, and that she certainly didn't need a shot. But the thermometer was still under her tongue, and a terrible tickling had erupted in her nose. It spread to her eyes and throat. It surged through her head and ripped from her mouth like an explosion.

"ACH . . . ACHOOOO! "

The thermometer shot from her mouth like a missile. It struck Dr. Hackler squarely between the eyes while a little rainstorm drenched him with germs.

After that, Mary didn't even protest when Dr. Hackler told her to roll up her sleeve for a shot.

As they left the examination room, a nurse called to Mary's mother.

"Mrs. Motley! Can I see you for a moment? We're planning this year's health fair at Mashville School and I need your help in a booth."

"Yes, of course," came the reply. "Mary, please wait for me in the front room. I'll only be a few minutes."

Mary rubbed her arm, sneezed, and entered the waiting room. All the chairs were filled. She sat on a little bench, covered with pillows, beside the princess. For awhile, neither of them spoke. Then Mary sneezed.

"Gross!" screamed the princess. "What's the big idea? I'm drenched! Don't you ever cover your mouth?"

"I'm sorry," said Mary. "I just can't catch them in time. I have a terrible cold, and I just had a shot for it."

"Well, look at me. I have a broken leg and now I'm covered with your spit."

"I'm sorry," Mary said again. "How did you break your leg?"

"I fell off the jungle gym. Well, actually, Vincent Von Roddersnot pushed me. He's a real creep."

Mary's nose suddenly tickled. She clenched her hands, closed her eyes, and opened her mouth. Just as the sneeze burst from her lips, she felt a pillow crash into her face. She sneezed into the pillow. Grabbing the pillow, she slowly lowered it. The princess, holding the other end, said "Well, at least we caught *that* one in time."

They looked at each other for a minute, then burst into giggles.

Mary and the princess talked together for a long time and Mary learned that her new friend's name was Joan Jones. Joan's father, Mary learned, had left when Joan was six months old. Her mother worked evenings at a nightclub, so Joan lived with her Aunt June. That's who she was awaiting now.

"She can't pick me up 'til she gets off work," sighed Joan. "She works 'til 5:30."

"I wish you could come home with me," said Mary. "But you'd catch my cold for sure. Maybe you could come after school next week."

"I s'pose I could," said Joan.

"Good! But just promise . . ." added Mary, "promise me that you won't push me off any more . . . any more . . . ACH . . . **ACHOOOO!"**

Mary and Joan became great friends. They played together each week, and Joan often spent Friday nights with the Motleys. One day as they walked to the park, Joan said, "Mary, why do you read your Bible every morning and go to church every Sunday? You're different from my other friends."

Mary was quiet for a moment. She felt scared, because she hadn't told many people about becoming a Christian. She didn't want to be laughed at or misunderstood. She didn't want to be asked hard questions. But she knew that God loved Joan. In fact, the Motleys' had been praying every night that Joan would become a Christian.

"I've asked Jesus to be my Savior," said Mary.

"What does that mean?"

"Well, it means that . . . Well, Joan, we all do bad things sometimes. We have meanness in our hearts. God loves us, though, and Jesus died to pay the penalty . . . Oh, I'm not sure I'm saying it right at all."

"I know that I've done some mean things," said Joan. "Remember when I pushed you off the slide?"

"I've done mean things too, Joan. We all have, but God wants to forgive us. The Bible says, *'For God so loved the world that He gave His one and only Son, that whoever believes in Him shall not perish but have eternal life.'* We can ask Him to forgive our sins and to be our Best Friend."

Then Mary had an idea. "Say," she said. "Why don't you go to church with us Sunday. I think you'd enjoy it, and you can learn more of what it means to become a Christian."

The next Sunday Joan was ready for church. She *did* like it, and she started going with the Motley's each week. Then one day about a month later, on a Sunday afternoon

_____

_____

_____

_____

_____

10. GROWING ON FROM HERE

Congratulations, you've finished!

By now you know what it means to become a Christian, and how Christians GROW. You should have memorized **John 3:16, Romans 6:4, 2 Peter 3:18,** and **Hebrews 10:25.** As time goes by, you'll want to memorize more and more verses. Why not start with some of those we've studied in these lessons? After memorizing each one, check it off and go on to the next one. And never forget—*God loves you so much that He gave His one and only Son, that you may believe in Him and not perish but have eternal life!*

_____ **Romans 3:23**

_____ **Romans 5:8**

_____ **Romans 6:23**

_____ **Matthew 7:24-27**

_____ **2 Timothy 3:16**

_____ **John 10:9-11**

_____ **John 14:15**

_____ **Colossians 3:16-17**

_____ **Colossians 3:20**

_____ **Acts 1:8**

Word Search Answer Key

P	R	A	I	S	E
R	Z	E	I	F	V
E	I	N	O	M	O
A	G	I	V	E	L
C	P	R	A	Y	B
H	N	R	A	E	L

Cross Word Puzzle Answer Key

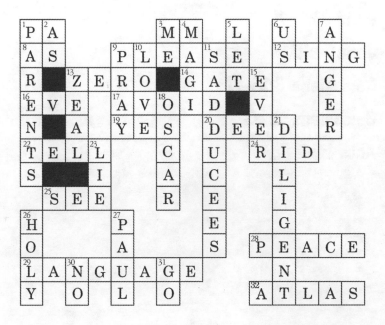